Yeti On The Loose

Yeti On The Loose

by

David MacPhail

www.stridentpublishing.co.uk

Published by
Strident Publishing Ltd
22 Strathwhillan Drive
The Orchard
Hairmyres
East Kilbride
G75 8GT

Tel: +44 (0)1355 220588
info@stridentpublishing.co.uk
www.stridentpublishing.co.uk

Published by Strident Publishing Limited, 2014
Text © David MacPhail, 2014
Cover art and design by Lawrence Mann (Lawrence Mann.co.uk)
Illustrations © Lawrence Mann, 2014

ISBN 978-1-905537-63-1

Typeset in Century Schoolbook by Andrew Forteath
Printed by Bell & Bain

The publisher acknowledges support from Creative Scotland towards the publication of this title.

Yetis are very odd creatures,
You cannot help gawp at their
features,
They're seven feet tall,
And hairy n'all,
They're almost as scary as teachers.

Chapter One

Great Uncle Jeremy

Great Uncle Jeremy was back from Nepal for the first time in ten years. Brian and Pippa Snotgrass and their Mum and Dad waved from the front door as his taxi appeared round the corner.

Dad had a huge fake grin plastered across his face.

"Keep smiling," he said. "Remember, no matter what he does or says you *must* be nice to him. It's his house we are living in."

Mum and Dad had agreed to house-sit for him when he first went away, and they'd been here ever since.

"We never thought he'd come back," said Mum through gritted teeth. "He could at least have had the decency to get eaten by something while he was out there."

A huge, ornate trunk was stuffed into the taxi's boot. It weighed down the whole back end of the car. The front wheels were hardly even touching the ground. Great Uncle Jeremy bulged out of the window, waving back at them with his stick.

"Ahoy there!" He flung open the door, stepped out of the car and bowed, flourishing a wide-brimmed hat with a leopard-skin trim. He looked every inch the adventurer, and there were rather a lot of inches.

With starey eyes, wild red hair and a thick overhanging brow there was something of the caveman about him. Which wasn't surprising. The caveman look was something that ran in the Snotgrass family. But Great Uncle Jeremy had the stariest, scariest eyes Brian had ever seen. As for the eyebrows, small rodents could nest in them. And if it wasn't for the monocle, and the fact he was talking, he could have been mistaken for an orang-utan in a safari suit.

He twiddled his long moustache, fixed his monocle in place and ogled the family suspiciously.

"So, you're the spongers who've been living in my house for all these years. Bah! Look at you. I've seen more life in a Sherpa's sock!"

Mum lunged at him. She had never liked the man, and now Brian could see why. Dad held her back, forcing out another fake laugh. "There there dear, don't get so excited. You can hug him later. Er, welcome, dear Uncle."

Dad tried to take the man by the arm and lead him inside, but Great Uncle Jeremy shrugged him off, jabbing his cane at the two children.

"Who are these two pygmies?"

Brian coughed. "I'm Brian."

"Brian eh," said Great Uncle Jeremy. "What an average name. And what do you want to be when you grow up, eh? An explorer like me?"

"No, actually, I want to be an inventor," said Brian. Although he wasn't sure he'd be a very good inventor. His past inventions included a fly escalator, a biscuit crumb collector and a rat magnetiser. His parents had barely forgiven him for that last one.

"Inventor indeed," snorted Great Uncle Jeremy. "Mouldering monsoons, I've seen more invention in a Darjeeling stoat!"

With that, he moved over to Brian's sister. She sucked her thumb and hid behind Mum as he bent over her. "What about you, you little weasel? What do you want to be?"

Probably a hippie, thought Brian, looking at her curly mane of hair and her 'Save the Rainforest' t-shirt. But she wouldn't answer, she just hid further behind her mother's skirt.

"Ha, ha! Never mind them," said Dad, and he pushed Brian and Pippa out of the way.

"Come inside, dear Uncle, and we'll make you a cup of tea."

"I know what I'd like to put in his tea," Mum muttered.

"Very good." Great Uncle Jeremy turned to the taxi driver, a sad, pathetic-looking man. "You there! Stop slouching! Carry my trunk into the house, there's a good fellow." The poor man nearly had a heart attack dragging it up the path.

"What have you got in 'ere? A gorilla?" he gasped.

Now it was Great Uncle Jeremy who laughed nervously. "Ha, ha! Gorilla indeed."

The taxi driver lugged the chest into the

hall. Then when he finally got his breath back he stood around waiting. "Ahem," he coughed.

"Ah, of course, a tip," said Great Uncle Jeremy. He fished inside his coat pocket. The taxi driver's eyes gleamed. Great Uncle Jeremy whipped something out. A two foot-long stuffed ferret. Or rather, a badly-stuffed ferret. Its tongue was hanging out and both its beady eyes were looking in opposite directions. Then he whacked it onto the man's outstretched palm.

"Wha-!" The taxi driver choked, looking down at the ferret's sad remains. "Whaddyou call this?"

"A Himalayan ferret. Now begone with you my man!"

"An 'imalayan what?" said the taxi driver. "You cheeky old git! I nearly broke my back liftin' that great 'orrible trunk in here. And you give me a dead animal as a tip! What sort of gratitude is that?"

"How dare you? Are you aware how much a Himalayan ferret will fetch in a Kathmandu market?"

"Bog off!" cried the taxi driver, and he

walloped the ferret down upon the trunk and walked out.

"You filthy piece of Yak dung! Come back here!" cried Great Uncle Jeremy, as the man jumped into his car and screeched off. Pippa tugged Brian's sleeve and whispered in his ear.

"What's this one saying?" cried Great Uncle Jeremy, prodding Pippa with his cane.

"Pippa says, aren't the Himalayas where the Abominable Snowman comes from?" said Brian.

"I think she means the Yeti," said Mum.

"A Yeti?" said Dad, who was just coming back in from the kitchen. "What's this about a Yeti?"

Great Uncle Jeremy's reaction was very peculiar. He let out a shriek. And he looked as if someone had just caught him red-handed nicking the King of Nepal's crown jewels.

Chapter Two

The Stuff of Legend

"Yeti... What Yeti? I don't know anything about a Yeti. It's not mine. It must have followed me here, I...."

"No," said Mum, looking at him as if he was mad. "Not here, of course, we mean in the Himalayas. That's where it comes from, isn't it?"

"Oh," said Great Uncle Jeremy. "Yes, I see what you mean now. Yes, that's where it comes from."

Pippa tugged Brian's sleeve and whispered into his ear again. She was always like this with strangers she didn't like. She would only speak to them through Brian.

"Pippa says have you ever seen one?"

Great Uncle Jeremy sat down on the trunk and mopped his brow with his hankie. A hankie that didn't look like it had been washed once in the last ten years.

"Ha!" he cried. "The Yeti is the stuff of

legend, a giant, hairy man–like creature said to live in the Himalayas. It's very shy, very secretive and mysterious. Very few people have even seen one, never mind captured one. Many have tried and failed." He leaned towards them and tapped the side of his nose. "Let's just say that whoever does capture a Yeti and brings him to the world will win fame and fortune beyond his wildest dreams!"

Great Uncle Jeremy jabbed Brian in the chest. "You. Help me carry my trunk down to the cellar."

Brian protested. "Eh? You must be joking. I'm not lugging that thing."

A look of panic flashed across Dad's face. He nudged Brian's head with his elbow. "Ha ha! He's just joking. Of course, he'd love to help you."

Brian sighed and picked up one end.

"Why do we have to drag it all the way down to the cellar?" said Brian, as they bumped it down the stairs one by one.

Great Uncle Jeremy's face was bright purple with effort.

"I want it safely stowed where no one can

touch him – er, I mean, it."

At last, they made it down the steps and dragged the trunk over to the back wall. Great Uncle Jeremy set his end down gently, but Brian dropped the other end with a bang.

Brian heard what sounded like a howl. A short, muffled one.

"What was that?" he said.

Great Uncle Jeremy suddenly stretched out his arms like a windmill and yawned. Or pretended to yawn. It was too big, too dramatic, to be anything but a pretend one. And he copied the howling noise. Or tried to.

It was obvious it wasn't the same noise. He sounded like a sea-lion at feeding time.

"What was what, old boy?" said Great Uncle Jeremy with a shifty look.

"I thought I heard a kind of howl, and it wasn't from you."

Great Uncle Jeremy was flustered now. Beads of sweat ran down his brow.

"Oh, it was probably nothing. It came from outside. It's just your imagination. Maybe it was the pipes."

"Nope," said Brian, stroking his chin. "Nope, it definitely came from the cellar." He stuck his ear to the trunk. "Hmm. In fact, it sounded like it came from inside here."

"Oh, *that* noise," Great Uncle Jeremy said. "Well, I can explain."

"Can you?"

"Well of course. It was, er… my watch." He held up his wrist and pulled back his sleeve. "See? Yes, this is a piece of prime Nepalese technology this. It has an alarm that howls. Every time it strikes the hour it goes off – HOWWWWL! Just like that."

This watch was like a museum piece. It was one step above a sundial. Brian doubted that the hands even went round.

"But the noise came from inside the trunk," Brian said. Great Uncle Jeremy's eyes were darting about like bluebottles trapped in a glass jar. "Ah, eh, yes....you see it's a special watch. I bought it from this ventriloquist in Outer Mongolia.....it's a ...ventriloquist watch. That's why it sounded like it came from inside the trunk."

Just as Brian was scratching his head, the cellar suddenly echoed with yet another howl. "You see," said Great Uncle Jeremy. "There it goes again. HOWWWWL!"

Brian looked at his own watch. "Hold on, it's twenty-three minutes past. I thought you said it went off at the hour?"

Great Uncle Jeremy grabbed him by the ear. "Ow!" cried Brian as he was dragged up the stairs.

"Er, it's still on Nepal time, that's why. Well, now that's sorted out let's get back up to the kitchen so you can make me that cup of tea and tell me all about yourself, eh?"

He slammed the cellar door behind them, locked the door and slipped the key inside his shirt pocket. "There. *My* cellar, and no one goes in there from now on but me," he said. Satisfied, he sat down at the kitchen table.

Pippa whispered over at Brian.

"What's he got in that trunk?"

"I don't know," replied Brian. "But I'm going to find out."

Chapter Three

Everything You Ever Needed To Know About The Snotgrass Family

Before we go any further, I need to tell you a bit more about the Snotgrasses.

The Snotgrasses are a big family. Brian and Pippa not only have one great uncle but they also have four great aunts, thirty-seven cousins and sixty-nine half cousins. Brian even had a pen pal from Bulgaria once who turned out to be a Snotgrass.

And, in two days time, there is going to be a big Snotgrass family wedding. That's the reason Great Uncle Jeremy gave for coming back from Nepal for the first time in ten years.

But, here's the best bit. Unlike you and me, the Snotgrass family did not evolve from monkeys. No. The Snotgrasses are different. Very different.

The Snotgrasses evolved from a bit of mouldy food that was trapped between a dinosaur's back teeth.

If you don't believe me then here's their family tree –

BIT OF MOULDY FOOD

The Snotgrass family tree

Mouldy bit of food trapped between
a dinosaur's front teeth

A piece of swimming snot
(*Snotgrass Flotius*)

A piece of crawling snot
(*Snotgrass Wobblius*)

A piece of walking snot
(*Snotgrass Erectus*)

Alexander the Great's chief goat-milker's
third dogsbody
(*Snotgrass Walkinaboutus*)

The Great Split

Dim Snotgrasses	*Clever Snotgrasses*
A piece of walking snot (again!)	Earls and Lords
Dung Salesmen	Inventors
Worm-farmers	Mad scientists
Fake poo makers	Astronauts
Teachers	Sea Captains
Great Uncle Jeremy	
	Brian and Pippa's Dad
Aunt Senga – Uncle Baz	Brian and Pippa

Tonga
    Fiji
        Samoa
            Skegness

Most of the Snotgrass family had failed to evolve beyond the caveman stage.

The exception was Brian and Pippa's side of the family. You see, at some point in the foggy depths of history the Snotgrasses split up. One half went one way, and one half went the other. One half are still as caveman-like as ever. Let's call them the Dim Snotgrasses. Great Uncle Jeremy is one of those. With his unruly hair, wild eyes, and overhanging forehead he is every inch a Dim Snotgrass.

But Brian and Pippa's side became clever. And they don't look like cavemen at all. As for Brian and Pippa themselves, they are in fact the farthest the Snotgrasses have ever evolved. They are at the very peak of the Snotgrass family tree and without a doubt the cleverest Snotgrasses who have ever lived.

Now, on with the story.....

Chapter Four

The Day Of The Wedding

That morning, Brian woke up with a jolt to find Pippa tugging at his leg.

"Uhh? Wassup?" said Brian.

"Something funny is going on," Pippa whispered.

"Eh?"

"I mean, with Great Uncle Jeremy."

"Tell me something I don't know." Brian turned over to go back to sleep. It was only half past eight and he wanted a lie in. He was knackered. His Uncle had caused him to run about like a maniac the night before. Polishing his boots, dusting his hat, hoovering his hankie, emptying out his toenail clippings. He even sent Brian down to the shops to buy corn plasters. All because Dad said they had to be nice to him no matter what.

But Pippa wouldn't leave him alone, she kept tugging. "Will you please go away!" he cried eventually.

"You see, he smells of dung," she said.

It was far from Brian to jump to the man's defence, but he had to correct his little sister on that.

"Great Uncle Jeremy smells of a lot of things: boot wax, wet dog and even baked beans, but one thing he doesn't smell of is dung. Okay?"

Then something very odd struck him. He opened his eyes and sniffed the air, sampling it like it was a fine wine. "Hang on, there *is* a dungy smell in this house."

"I told you," said Pippa.

Brian threw back the covers. Together, he and Pippa crept down the stairs, sniffing all the way. The smell got stronger as they neared the cellar door.

"What could it be?" Brian sniffed at the keyhole and peeked through the crack underneath the door.

"Do you know what else?" said Pippa. "As soon as Mum and Dad went to work this morning I saw him creep into the kitchen and steal all the fruit from the fruit bowl. He sneaked down to the cellar with it. And when he came back up a minute later all the fruit was gone."

Sure enough, when Brian went into the kitchen to check, there wasn't a single bit of fruit left. "Do you know where he is now?"

"In the garden," said Pippa. "He's been out there for ages. He's been on the phone. I think he's speaking to a man from a newspaper."

Brian edged open the kitchen door. Their great uncle was standing at the foot of the garden, next to the garage, but had such a loud voice that he could still be heard.

"I'm telling you, Mr Editor, it's the story of the century," he was saying. "You'll see that I'm right when I unveil it to you at the wedding."

Story of the century? What could it all mean? One thing was for sure, Great Uncle Jeremy hadn't just come back for a wedding. Great Uncle Jeremy was up to something.

"We've got to get the key to the cellar," said Brian.

"But, how?" said Pippa. "It's in his shirt pocket."

"Okay," Brian said, thinking. "We either pick his pocket or get him to take off his shirt."

Pippa screwed up her face. "Yuck! Can't we just wait 'till he takes a bath?"

"That's it, a bath! Genius!" he said, grabbing his sister and spinning her around. "But, we don't have to wait until bath time. Follow me, I've got a plan."

Brian led his sister back upstairs. In the top drawer of the cabinet next to his bed lay his most prized possessions. These included his harmonica, his box of fishing flies, and, best of all, a carton of itching powder he'd brought back from a holiday in Blackpool. "Stay right here and watch this."

He left Pippa at the bedroom window and ran back down the stairs, sneaking out of the kitchen door into the garden. He crept up the ivy that clung to the garden wall, and then crawled onto the roof of the garage.

Great Uncle Jeremy was standing right underneath. He was still talking to the newspaper editor. "Why the wedding? My

whole family will be there of course. I want them all to see it. They never thought I'd amount to anything. Ha! Well I'll show them. I'll show them all. The fools!"

Brian flipped open the top of the carton and carefully sprinkled the fine white dust over his uncle's head.

As the cloud of itching powder covered him, he stopped talking and looked up. Just in time, Brian ducked back under cover.

"What in the name of Suffering Tibet is this?" he cried.

Brian climbed back down the ivy and into the house. When he got upstairs Pippa was still watching from the window, waiting eagerly for something to happen.

Brian hummed, flopped onto the bed and picked up a comic.

"It didn't work," said Pippa after a moment. "He just dusted himself off and started talking again."

Brian yawned and looked at his watch. "Five, four, three, two, one….." All of a sudden Great Uncle Jeremy roared, and it was so loud the glass in the windows shuddered.

"WAAAAAAAAAAAAAHHHHHHH!"

He dropped the phone and started jumping up and down. It looked like he was being attacked by a swarm of killer bees. "Great Everest! Someone please help me!"

"What did I tell you?" said Brian.

Their Uncle ran into the house and leapt up the stairs, scratching himself all over.

"Aaargh! Oooh! Gerroff! Bathroom, I must get to the bathroom!" He ripped off his shirt, then slammed the bathroom door shut behind him and turned on the shower.

"Hah! My plan was perfect," said Brian. He yanked one of the plastic flowers from a nearby vase. Then he flipped it round and used it to pick up the shirt. He slipped his fingers inside the breast pocket and picked out the cellar door key. "There we go. That itching powder will take at least ten minutes to wear off. By the time Great Uncle Jeremy has finished in the bathroom, we'll have found out what's in the cellar. This key will be back in his shirt pocket and he'll be none the wiser."

Chapter Five

What's in the cellar?

Brian led Pippa down the dark cellar steps.

"I've changed my mind. I don't want to see what's in the trunk," she said, shivering.

"Don't be scared," said Brian, who was just as scared but didn't want to show it. "It could be treasure."

Pippa's hand was clamped over her nose now. "Treasure that smells of poo! I don't think so."

Brian shrugged. "Maybe he found it in a dung pit."

"What kind of idiot puts treasure in a dung pit?" said Pippa.

"A Snotgrass idiot?"

Suddenly the trunk lurched across the floor. They froze.

"Wha.... What kind of treasure does that?" said Pippa, moving a step closer to her brother who moved a step closer to the stairs. The lid of the trunk started banging, like it was going to come loose. "Quick," he cried. "Jump on top of it!"

Brian leapt onto the trunk and grabbed hold of the lock on the front, trying to hold himself steady. It came loose with a terrible clunk.

"What have you done?" cried Pippa.

The lid of the trunk sprang open and Brian was thrown off. Then the front popped loose and slammed onto the floor. Pippa gasped. Brian yelled.

They could hardly believe what they were looking at.

There, sitting cross-legged in a bed of hay, sat a huge man. Or was it an ape? His face looked quite human. But he had long arms, big feet and was covered in reddish brown hair.

One hand was holding a half-eaten banana. The other was scratching his head.

For a second, all Brian and Pippa could do was stare. Stare at this strange and curious creature. And for his part all the ape-man could do was stare back. And chew his banana.

Then Pippa opened her mouth and let out

a loud, terrifying scream.

"EEEEEAAAAAAAAAAGGGHHHHH! A monster!"

Brian started screaming too. "A monster! It's a MONSTER!"

Both of them were screaming at the top of their lungs.

The creature panicked. He jumped up into the air, throwing his arms about and bashing himself on the head. "AAAAAAAAGH!"

Then he saw the crack of light from the top of the stairs and made a break for it. As he fled, his arms dragged behind him, bouncing off each step as he went.

Brian grabbed his sister by the shoulders. "He's gone now. It's okay."

Pippa couldn't stop shaking. "It was a monster!" she yelled. "A big, hairy monster."

Brian gripped her hand. "Come on," he whispered.

Slowly, they crept back up the steps. Brian's heart was thumping. Any second now he was expecting the creature to leap out at them and attack.

"I'm scared, Brian," Pippa kept saying. She was almost in tears.

"So am I,' he admitted and they held hands even tighter.

They peeked out of the cellar door. Nothing. All was quiet.

They tiptoed along the hallway towards the living room. Brian pushed open the door and they glanced inside.

The creature was lying on the floor with his head and the top half of his body hidden under the rug. All they could see sticking out were his legs and his big hairy bottom, which was quivering with fear. They could hear him whimpering under there.

"Aw," said Pippa, who all of a sudden wasn't terrified any more. "The poor thing. He thinks because he can't see us then we can't see him. That's what I used to do when I was really little."

Pippa went to the other end of the rug, lifted it up and crept underneath. "What are you doing? Are you nuts?" cried Brian.

He watched as Pippa wriggled her way towards the ape man.

"Boo!"

The creature screamed. It almost burst Brian's ear drums. Then he jumped up and ran around the room, terrified. The rug was still attached to him, hanging around his shoulders like a cloak. He leapt on top of chairs, he ran up and down the dining table. He looked a bit like Superman, in fact. A very hairy Superman.

"We have to do something!" Brian yelled. "He'll be swinging from the lights next." He spoke too soon, as the creature leapt into the air and grabbed the big overhead light. He only managed to swing for a second before it, along with half the ceiling, ripped out and crashed to the ground. "He's wrecking the place. What are we going to do?"

"Don't worry, I've got an idea." Pippa ran into the kitchen and returned with a big bag of cashew nuts. She unfolded the packet and held it out to the creature. "Would you like some nuts?"

The creature stopped screaming. He ogled her for a moment. Pippa didn't move. She just smiled and moved the bag closer to him. "Nuts," she kept saying. "Mmmmm." The creature looked at the nuts.

He stepped towards her. He angled his head forward and sniffed the bag. Then, in a blink

of an eye he grabbed it. It was a nifty move, but a bit too nifty for the plastic bag, which burst open, scattering nuts everywhere. The creature yelped with excitement. He ran round like a maniac picking them all up.

"Mmmm!" he said, stuffing them into his mouth and spitting them all over the place. "Mmmmmmm! NUTS!"

"What are we going to do?" said Brian. "Great Uncle Jeremy will kill us for this."

"No he won't," said Pippa. "Don't you know what he's doing? Don't you realise what this poor creature is? It's a Yeti. Our great uncle has smuggled this poor Yeti back from Nepal so he can show it to the world and become rich and famous."

Brian scratched his head. His little sister was clearly one step ahead of him here.

"But I thought Yetis didn't exist. They're a legend," he said.

"Well that's rubbish, it's no myth," said Pippa. "And the proof is standing right in front of you. Can you imagine what it'll be like when the newspapers find out? All those cameras flashing away, all those people staring at him. And then he'll be taken to a zoo and prodded and stared at for the rest of his life. The poor thing." Pippa picked up the Yeti's hand and started stroking it. He grinned back and spat some more nuts over her. "We have to save him. We just have to."

"Save him?" said Brian. "And how do you suppose we do that?"

Brian had a vision of the two of them hitch-hiking all the way over the Hindu Kush mountains carrying the Yeti in a rucksack. They'd never get permission to go to Nepal on their own. Not in a million years. Brian's mother was a worrier. She wouldn't even let him go on the escalator at Tesco.

"It's a long long way to the Himalayas," said Brian, trying to ignore the Yeti, who had finished the nuts and was now eating the curtains.

"You'll think of a plan though," said Pippa. "You always do. You're good with plans. We need to hide him, keep him a secret, keep him away from Great Uncle Jeremy."

Before Brian could put his brain in gear, the Yeti noisily spat out the shreds of curtain. It was clear from his screwed up expression that he did not like the taste of polyester. He leapt to his feet and yelled.

"NUTS!"

In a flash, the Yeti smashed through the French windows, sending glass and wood flying all over the garden.

"Quick! Stop him!" said Brian, but even as he said it he knew it was too late. The Yeti jumped on top of the garage, galloped along the roof, and then disappeared over the garden wall.

Chapter Six

A Yeti On The Loose!

Brian dashed upstairs. He pulled his clothes on over his pyjamas before stuffing his sister into a pair of jeans and a t-shirt. Just in case, he grabbed his pocket money too.

They tiptoed past the bathroom, stopping briefly to listen at the door

Great Uncle Jeremy was still in the shower. He'd succeeded in washing off all the itching powder. Now he was enjoying himself, singing *Daydream Believer* at the top of his voice. He made it sound less like a pop song and more like Tibet's national anthem. Maybe it *was* Tibet's national anthem.

"He'll be on our trail as soon as he realises what's happened, so we'd better find the Yeti quick," said Brian.

They followed the Yeti's trail over the garden wall. In the lane behind the garage, one of the neighbours, Mr Coombs, was hanging out of his car window, crying. And there was the Yeti, bouncing up and down on the roof of the car with a look of glee on his face.

"Run for your lives!" yelled Mr Coombs as the roof caved in on him. "There's an ape man on the loose!"

The Yeti leapt off the roof of the car and galloped down the lane. Brian and Pippa set off in pursuit. But the Yeti was too fast for them. He soon disappeared round the corner.

When they arrived at the junction with the main road they were both out of breath.

"Which way did he go?" gasped Pippa. But Brian didn't need to answer. One look up the high street said it all.

Two cars had swerved and crashed into each other, steam hissing from their crushed engines. A huge German Shepherd dog sprinted past them at full speed, whimpering. Its owner was being dragged along behind it, yelling, "Sit, Bomber, sit!" The postman was hiding up a telegraph pole, shaking like a – well, like a man who has just seen a Yeti.

Further down the street another man was cowering on the roof of his shed. His garden looked like a bomb had hit it. His flower bed was completely destroyed, and his vegetable patch had been ripped up.

"Help!" he cried, tottering on the rickety rooftop. "There's an orang-utan on the rampage! It stole all my rhubarb and ate my begonias. I'm never going to win Garden of the Month now."

"Look, there he is," said Brian. In the distance they could see the Yeti bounding over the car rooftops towards the town centre.

Brian and Pippa ran after him. "Hey! Aren't you going to help me down?" cried the man as they disappeared. "I'm scared of heights."

"Sorry. We have to stop him before he gets to the town centre!" said Brian as they ran. But it was too late. The Yeti was already there.

As Brian and Pippa arrived at the shopping precinct they could hear the sound of smashing glass coming from the TV shop.

A woman screamed. The shop staff burst out of the door, running for their lives.

"Help! It's a gorilla! He's the size of King Kong. "

Inside the shop, Brian and Pippa found him at last, hanging from the ceiling, watching the rows and rows of televisions which lined the wall. They were all showing the same programme. The Yeti bounced up and down and made lots of excited yelping noises. It was David Attenborough's wildlife show. Chimpanzees were swinging through the trees in a jungle in Africa.

"Huuuu! Huffrrr Uffrr! DAVID ATTENBOROUGH!" he cried. "Huffrr Uffrr! MONKEEES!"

"Yeti!" cried Pippa in a firm voice. "Yeti, come down here this instant!"

The Yeti gave a hoot of delight and then jumped down onto the floor. He bounced over, took Pippa by the hand and grinned at her.

"NUTS!" he cried.

"You want more nuts?" said Pippa. "Then come with us. And behave yourself this time!"

Brian and Pippa led him back out into the street.

"Good work," said Brian. "Now, let's get him home without drawing any more attention to ourselves."

That wasn't going to be easy. Two women dropped their shopping and screamed. That pretty much did it. Before they knew it people were fainting, running for their lives, barricading themselves inside shops. One man even jumped into a wheelie bin and closed the lid on himself. The Yeti was causing total mayhem.

"Help! Run! Quick, get the police! An ape! Some sort of ape has escaped from the zoo!"

Brian needed to think fast if he was going to get them out of this. And the answer wasn't far away. It was right next to them, in fact. Gianni's Hair Salon. Underneath the sign on the front of the shop there was a caption:

I take pride in creating beauty....I can create a masterpiece of anyone's hair

"That's it!" He grabbed Pippa, fished out his pocket money and dumped some of it into her hand.

"What's this for?" she said. He turned her around and pointed her in the direction of the charity shop.

"It's my new plan. Go in there and get him some clothes."

"Brilliant idea! A disguise." Pippa dashed inside. Brian grabbed the Yeti's hand and dragged him into the hair salon.

Inside, a row of posh ladies were having their hair done. As Brian and the Yeti entered and the stench of dung wafted through the shop, the women's noses all turned up.

"Euch! What is that awful smell?" said one snooty-looking lady.

They all looked up and saw the Yeti. There was a moment of stunned silence, before one of them screamed.

"AAAAGH! It's a monster!"

This set off a huge panic. The ladies threw off their gowns. They wrestled each other out of the way, running to escape out the back door, their hair-dos half finished. Some of them were still attached to the big hair drying machines. One woman looked up just as the hairdresser began squirting styling mousse into her hair. She got it in her eyes instead. She ran round the salon, arms stretched out in front of her, before disappearing into the broom cupboard, where she crashed into something large and metallic and knocked herself out.

Only one person remained after the ladies had escaped: Gianni, the owner of the salon. He was a big man with an equally big hairstyle. The hairdresser dropped his tongs into a basin of water.

"Can I help you?" he gulped.

"Er, can my friend have a shave, please?" replied Brian.

Chapter Seven

The Famous Gianni

Gianni was insulted.

"Wait a minute," he cried as the Yeti climbed up onto the chair and started jumping up and down. "I am a professional hair stylist, I do not do smelly apes!"

"Oh please," said Brian. "Can't you help?"

"No, absolutely not," cried Gianni.

Brian looked around at the walls of the salon. They were covered with pictures of Gianni with famous people. There was him and Ralph Stallion, the famous actor, and Egbert Dinkerhunk, the singer. This was a man with a big reputation.

"Think of the challenge though." Brian nodded over at the pictures. "I bet no other famous stylist in the World has done a real Yeti before."

"Yeti?" replied the hairdresser. "He's a Yeti?"

"It says outside that you take pride in creating beauty. Well, this'll be your finest ever creation. We'll even let you take a photo for your collection."

A sparkle lit up inside the hairdresser's eyes. Meanwhile the Yeti leapt onto the counter, picked up a tube of hair gel and squidged it all over his own face. "And, besides, if you don't do something quick he's going to make an awful mess."

Now Gianni was taken by the idea.

"Of course! It's fantastic! The greatest challenge for any artist. I will create beauty out of the ape!"

As if the Yeti wanted to thank him, he grabbed Gianni and started slobbering all over him. "Think nothing of it," Gianni said.

Immediately, he set to work. He got out his clippers and started shaving off the creature's long, tangly locks. The Yeti chuckled as the clippers tickled him behind the ears. As Gianni moved up and down his neck and round his chin, his giggling got even worse.

"Hoa-ho-ho....Hffrrufrrr

....MONKEEEEEEEESSS!"

By the time Pippa came running in from the charity shop, carrying a big brown suit on a hanger, a huge pile of red hair lay on the

salon floor.

"He's going to be the best dressed Yeti in the World." She pulled the trousers onto him and then stuffed his arms inside a shirt. She'd even managed to buy an old kipper tie, which she fastened round his neck.

Gianni was concentrating very hard on creating a work of art for the Yeti's hairstyle. Beads of sweat trickled down his forehead as he rubbed gel in to the creature's hair and then combed it carefully.

When Gianni finished the Yeti stood up. Brian and Pippa could hardly believe it. The transformation was amazing. Gianni had given the Yeti a total makeover. The haircut made him look smart, even stylish. And apart from those big feet of his and the long arms sticking out of the cuffs of his jacket, he looked almost human.

"Fantastic!" said Gianni. "What a work of genius! I will get my camera."

Brian took a photo of the hairdresser standing with his arm around the Yeti. Gianni then lovingly pinned it up on the wall, giving it pride of place amongst the famous people. Hand in hand, Brian, Pippa,

and their new-look Yeti left the Salon.

Four police cars had arrived on the high street, and a crowd of people had gathered. News had got about that an ape-man was loose in the town centre, and everybody wanted to find out if it was true.

The police were standing about taking notes. "Okay, so where is this ape man?" they were asking.

Brian held his breath and squeezed tighter on the Yeti's hand. The three of them walked past completely unnoticed.

"Phew! It looks like our plan has worked," said Brian as they turned the corner. "But keep hold of his hand just in case he tries to run off again."

"What are we going to do now?" said Pippa. But Brian didn't have a moment to think.

"Galloping Glaciers! You there!"

Great Uncle Jeremy was running towards them. He was wearing his wedding suit.

"Oh no!" said Pippa. "How are we going to get out of this?"

Chapter Eight

Oh No, Not Yeti!

Brian was about to run for it, but it was no use. He was too close.

"You there!" Great Uncle Jeremy grabbed him by the arm. "I caught you. It was you who put itching powder down my back, wasn't it? You crafty little beggar. Lucky I had my wedding suit ready, that's all. Otherwise all I would have to wear today would be your father's dressing gown and a pair of pink flip-flops."

"Leave us alone!" cried Brian.

"No. Why should I? You took my key whilst I was in the shower! You opened the cellar door! You looked in my trunk. And, most important of all, you stole my Yeti!"

Pippa tugged Brian's sleeve and whispered something in his ear.

"She said he's not your Yeti" said Brian. "He doesn't belong to anyone."

"Oh no? I captured it. I smuggled it here

in the trunk. Of course it's mine. It's going to bring me fame and fortune, so you'd better tell me where it is."

He suddenly noticed that they were holding hands with a large man in a suit whom he didn't recognise. He looked the Yeti up and down very closely. "Who is this person?"

Brian realised that their short-sighted Uncle didn't have his monocle in.

"Er…. Who is he? Good question, er…" Brian tried to think of something but his mind went blank.

"Come come. Speak up for yourself," said Great Uncle Jeremy to the Yeti. "What's your name, man?"

Pippa gave the Yeti's hand a squeeze. Amazingly, the Yeti spoke back.

"DAVID ATTENBOROUGH!" he slobbered.

"Attenborough, eh? Pleased to meet you," said Great Uncle Jeremy.

"NUTS!" cried the Yeti.

"What?" said the Uncle. "Of all the cheek! I've never been spoken to like this in all my life. Who taught you your manners, sir?"

"MONKEYS!" cried the Yeti.

"I quite believe it. But, I don't have time for this nonsense. I want my Yeti back and I'm not going to let you two go until you give it to me."

Now he grabbed hold of Pippa too. Brian remembered that he still had half a tube of itching powder in his pocket. He fished it out, flipped it open and poured what was left of it right down the back of his Uncle's neck.

"What? Gerroff!" Brian and Pippa fell to the ground. Their Uncle clutched his back, realising he'd been caught out for a second time. "Curse my Crampons! Not again!"

Suddenly, he froze solid.

"What's happening?" said Pippa. A colossal earthquake was building underneath the man's clothes.

"It's a double dose," said Brian. "This time it's going to hit him much quicker." It was as if a huge volcano was exploding. "AAAAAAAAAAAAAAAAAGGGGGHHHH !"

He jumped up and down. He screamed at the top of his voice, reaching his hands down the neck of his shirt, frantically trying to itch his back. It looked like a tribal war dance. So much so in fact that the Yeti started jumping up and down too, copying Great Uncle Jeremy's every move.

"AAAAAAAAAAAAAAAAAAGGGGGH-HHH !" cried the Yeti, nodding his head with excitement. He thought he was dancing along.

Great Uncle Jeremy was going berserk. He rampaged back up the street. As he ran

he tore off all his clothes and chucked them away, until he was dressed only in a gigantic pair of white underpants. He leapt over a fence, his enormous flabby belly jiggling about like a blancmange. Then he disappeared into the trees.

Brian and Pippa were rolling about in fits of laughter. They couldn't get up, they could hardly even breathe.

Suddenly, Pippa stopped laughing. She looked up, and clasped her hands over her mouth.

"Brian! The Yeti's gone!"

They'd been laughing so hard they'd completely forgotten that the Yeti was copying Great Uncle Jeremy. So when their

Uncle had turned and run off, the Yeti had turned and run off too, but in the other direction – back into the town, which was now crowded with people. They'd all come out hoping to catch a glimpse of this ape-man that everyone was talking about. Brian and Pippa couldn't see the creature anywhere.

"I can't believe it! We've lost him again!" said Brian.

Chapter Nine

I'm Not Finished Yeti

They looked for the Yeti everywhere. They went down to the junction, they went right, they went left, they went right again, then they walked round the block until finally they returned to the junction again.

"Where could he have gone?" said Brian.

Pippa shrieked as she looked at her watch.

"Look at the time. We've got to get back. The wedding, remember?"

"But what about the Yeti? We can't just leave him wandering around town on his own."

"Well, if he can survive the Himalayas I'm sure he'll survive our town centre," replied Pippa. "And, anyway, Mum and Dad will kill us if we're late. Come on."

As they made their way home they both kept looking back, hoping to see the Yeti galloping up behind them. But, there was no sign of him. They arrived home in a miserable mood.

"Is Great Uncle Jeremy here?" said Pippa to Dad as they came through the door.

"There you are," said Dad, vacuuming the living room floor. "We were worried sick about you. No, we've not seen him all day, and a good thing too, 'cos your mother wants to kill him. Did you see the mess he left this place in? Now, come on and get dressed. We're going to be late as it is!"

With that, Dad rushed them both upstairs to get ready. By the time they left, half an hour later, Great Uncle Jeremy was still nowhere to be seen.

The wedding was to be held in a big marquee at the house of Aunt Senga and Uncle Baz.

Aunt Senga and Uncle Baz and their family were 'dim' Snotgrasses. They were also incredibly rich. I know what you are thinking: how can they be rich if they are so dim? Well, Uncle Baz won the lottery, that's how. Any dimwit can win the lottery.

They were the snobbiest, most horrible people you could ever meet. They wanted everyone to see how much money they had.

They were determined to have the biggest, poshest wedding the town had ever seen. The wedding party included six bridesmaids, five best men, fourteen ushers, five page boys and eight flower girls.

Aunt Senga and Uncle Baz had four daughters. Each daughter was named after a favourite holiday destination. There was Tonga, Fiji, Samoa, and Skegness. Cousin Tonga was the one getting married.

Brian and Pippa and their Mum and Dad arrived at the wedding in the nick of time. They would have been much later if Mum had got her way. She was so angry with Great Uncle Jeremy she wanted to stop and buy a knuckle duster.

They parked the car and rushed to the marquee just as the ceremony was about to begin. Tonga and her sisters were waiting outside the entrance. Tonga was the ugliest bride Brian had ever seen. She looked like a caveman wearing a dress.

"Oh no, not you lot!" she screeched, taking her chewing gum out of her mouth and sticking it to the side of the tent. "We was hoping you wasn't coming."

"Sorry we're late," said Dad, tucking his shirt into his trousers.

"We knew this would happen," snapped one of the other sisters, Fiji. "Tonga wanted her wedding to be perfect, and you lot just wanna ruin it, don't ya!"

Brian thought that was a bit of a cheek considering Fiji hadn't even shaved for the occasion.

"Sorry," said Dad, and he pushed Brian and Pippa inside.

The interior of the marquee was bedecked in flowers. On one side there was a long buffet table piled high with food and drink, including an enormous punch bowl, a champagne fountain and a giant platter of *vol-au-vents*. On the other side, a stage had been set up for the band. Red velvet curtains were drawn across the front of the stage.

Another of Brian and Pippa's Uncles, Uncle George, came up to them to say hello. He had a beer belly and a big red face, probably through all the laughing he did. Brian didn't know anyone who laughed as much as him.

"Ha! You know, the funniest thing happened when I was in town earlier on,"

said Uncle George. "I was on my way here
and happened to bump into your Great Uncle
Jeremy. Ha!"

"Ah, so he did make it, then?" said Dad.
Brian thought that this was odd, since Great
Uncle Jeremy definitely hadn't been back to
the house when they left and he'd chucked

away his wedding suit because of the itching powder.

"You know, I'd never met Jeremy before. Ha! I saw this fellow walking down the street. Straight away, I looked at him and I said to myself, 'As I live and breathe, that man is a Snotgrass. Back from Nepal after all these years.' So, anyway I brought him here on the bus. He doesn't say much, mind you, but what a joker!"

Brian and Pippa looked at each other. It didn't sound like the bad-tempered Uncle Jeremy they knew. He wouldn't know a joke if it got up and gave him a haircut.

"Where is he?" said Dad, looking around.

Uncle George pointed through the crowd. At the other end of the marquee, wearing an old brown suit and a kipper tie, stood the Yeti. He'd just taken a bite out of the flower display.

"Yeti!" cried Pippa, and she and Brian ran over to him.

"Hfffr ufffrrr. NUTS!" cried the Yeti when he saw them, and he gave them both a huge hug which almost made their eyes pop out. Pippa took the flowers away from him, and

David MacPhail

they led him over to the seats.

"We've got to keep him quiet during the ceremony," said Brian. "Or else we're in for it."

Pippa agreed, but they should have known better. Trying to keep a Yeti quiet and in his seat during a wedding, or during anything for that matter, is more difficult than trying to teach the Loch Ness Monster how to knit.

The wedding began with the bridal march. But instead of organ music, Tonga's walk down the aisle was accompanied by a bagpiper playing the theme music to *EastEnders*. The Yeti caused a bit of a stir when he started howling along to the tune.

Tonga glared over at them. "Tell him to shut up!" Brian clapped his hands over the Yeti's mouth, but it only seemed to make the noise worse. It was as if there were a mugging going on. Uncle George looked round at them and laughed.

"What a joker! Ha!" he said.

When the Vicar said, "If anyone has any objections to this wedding speak now or forever hold your peace," the Yeti leaned over and let loose a colossal blast of air from his

bottom. All the women in the tent screamed.
Tonga's mum, Aunt Senga, nearly fainted.

Uncle Baz turned round and yelled. "Will you shut up, whoever you are! I'm trying to get rid of my daughter here!"

When the ceremony finished the bride picked up a microphone and began screeching along to a karaoke version of Whitney Houston's *I Will Always Love You*. "AYE-EE-AYE WILL ALWAYS LAAAVV YOU-EE-OO-OO-OO-OO!" Her new husband looked horrified, as if he'd just realised what he'd got himself into by marrying this woman.

It was all too much for the Yeti. He clutched his ears and howled. He shook Pippa off and jumped up onto the buffet table, landing on the platter of *vol-au-vents*. He tried to run, but kept slipping. His legs spun round like Catherine wheels, machine-gunning dozens of tiny *vol-au-vents* into the sitting guests. Then he shot along the table on all fours, squashing cakes and blancmanges along the way. He stopped only to dunk his head into the punchbowl and drink from it in big slobbery gulps. Then he catapulted into the champagne fountain, spraying glass and champagne all over the vicar.

The whole tent was in uproar. Tonga

dropped her bouquet of flowers and started screaming.

"Aaagh! Mum! He's ruining it!"

"Ha! He'll do anything for a joke, that Uncle of yours!" cried Uncle George as he bent double with laughter.

Now the Yeti leapt onto the ground and began to eat Tonga's bouquet. Tonga's Mum really did faint this time. In the confusion, Brian and Pippa grabbed the creature and dragged him outside. They had to make sure he ducked his head, or they would have taken the whole marquee with them.

"What are we going to do now?" said Pippa. "We've ruined the wedding."

"It's alright," said Brian. "I've got a plan. We'll put him in Dad's car until later. Then, when things have calmed down a bit, we'll sneak out, take the Yeti back to the house and put him back in the cellar."

Brian returned to the tent to ask his dad if he could borrow the car keys. Then the two of them rushed the Yeti to the car. They crammed him into the front seat, his head squashed against the roof and his enormous tree-trunk legs sticking up over the dashboard. The Yeti's eyes lit up as he looked at the controls.

"Hffrr uffrr!" he said, and he started playing with the steering wheel.

"We'll be back soon," said Pippa, locking the car door.

"Phew! At least that's one problem out the way," said Brian.

Just as they were about to go back inside the marquee, a pair of big, hairy hands gripped the two of them by the shoulders, hoisted them in the air and then dumped them on the ground.

Great Uncle Jeremy was standing over them, his monocle twitching furiously. He was wearing Dad's blue dressing gown and a pair of pink flip-flops. The ends of his moustache were trembling with rage.

"Where's my Yeti, you pair of Yaks!"

Chapter Ten

Are We Nearly There Yeti?

Brian took a moment to recover from the shock. "Come on!" said Great Uncle Jeremy. "I know you've got it."

If he was expecting them to surrender quietly he was wrong. Pippa sprang to her feet and stamped on his toes. "Don't try to bully us, you big fat bully!"

"OW! Ow! Ow! Ow!" He hopped up and down. "So she can talk now, can she?"

"I'm not scared of you anymore!"

"Listen here, you meddling little rodents! If you don't return my Yeti this instant I will go in there and explain to your whole family how *you* ruined the wedding."

"We didn't ruin the wedding!" said Brian. "It was the Yeti."

"You were the ones who let it out of the trunk. It was all because of you."

Pippa glared at Great Uncle Jeremy. "You took the Yeti away from its home in the

Himalayas! You brought it here in the first place, you big walrus!"

Now their Uncle juddered with rage, and his eye twitched so much that his monocle cracked. His lip stiffened and he leaned right into their faces.

"The national press is going to be here in twenty minutes," he said. "I am going to stand on that stage in there and reveal the creature to the world. And you are going to help me. Got that?"

"Or what?" said Pippa.

"I'll tell you what," said Great Uncle Jeremy. "If you don't help me I'll kick you and your Mum and Dad out of my house. How would you like that, eh? How would you like to be homeless, to live on the streets?"

"You can't do that!" cried Pippa.

"Oh, yes I can. Remember, it's my house you're living in. And if I want to throw you out I can."

Brian and Pippa were so shocked they could hardly speak. This was blackmail. Great Uncle Jeremy gave a triumphant laugh. "Ha! That's right. A nice little eviction. Just make sure that the creature is behind

the curtain on the stage in five minutes time,
if you know what's good for you."

He looked at his watch. "Well, must dash,
old fruits. Fame and fortune await. Let me
know when it's done."

Brian and Pippa watched him flip-flop
his way into the tent. They sat down on the
wall and tried to think of a way out of the

mess, but no matter how hard they tried they couldn't.

"There's nothing else for it," said Brian. "He's beaten us. We'll have to give the Yeti back. If we don't, Great Uncle Jeremy will make us homeless."

"Oh, the poor Yeti," said Pippa. "For the rest of his life he's going to be photographed and put in a cage and prodded. I'll bet you right now all he wants to do is go home to the peace and quiet of the Himalayas."

"Yup," agreed Brian. "The poor thing."

Downcast, the two of them returned to the car to fetch the Yeti.

They weren't surprised to find that the car was rocking from side to side. The alarm was going off, the boot and the bonnet had both flipped open and the stereo was thumping out loud music.

Inside, the Yeti was bouncing about like a maniac, hooting with joy and bashing his head on the car roof.

"So much for peace and quiet," said Brian. "Quick, get him out of there. Dad will kill us if he sees this."

Just then, the airbag inflated and the Yeti

was squashed against the seat.

"Uuuh! Hffrr uffrrr!" he cried, from underneath.

They had to wait until the airbag deflated before they could try to pull him out. But the Yeti didn't want to leave. He'd got quite attached to the car. He held tight onto the steering wheel while Brian and Pippa tugged at his legs. It was only when Pippa started tickling him under the arms that he finally let go.

"Right, let's get this over with," said Brian.

They sneaked the Yeti back inside the tent, then onto the stage and behind the curtain. There were tears in Pippa's eyes as she hugged him tight."Oh, Yeti, I'm really sorry. Really, we tried our best," she said. The Yeti smiled back.

"Hffrr uffrr…. Pip-pa," he said.

"That's right," replied Pippa. "Pippa's my name. Well done! You know, for an Abominable Snowman you're not really all that abominable. Very nice, in fact."

They gave the Yeti a bunch of flowers to eat, and then Brian and Pippa slipped through the curtains to find their great uncle.

Photographers and reporters from the national press were now pouring into the marquee, creating a storm of noise and confusion. Nobody at the wedding knew why they were there. Tonga thought they were from OK Magazine and were there to photograph her.

Only Great Uncle Jeremy knew what was really happening. He stepped onto the stage, stood in front of the curtain and looked around the tent with a smug grin.

"I love it when one of my plans works out."

He gave Brian and Pippa a triumphant wink. Pippa blew him a raspberry.

"Ladies and gentlemen!" he cried. The reporters and photographers crowded round the stage and a hush descended inside the marquee.

"Right!" Mum tore off her jacket and tossed it at Dad, along with her handbag and shoes. "That's it! I'm going to throttle him." Dad almost had a hernia holding her back.

"A man in a dressing gown, ha!" laughed Uncle George. "This wedding gets better by the minute!"

"I have an announcement to make," continued Great Uncle Jeremy. "I have spent ten years searching the Himalayas for the famous Abominable Snowman, the legendary Yeti. Some said that I was foolish. Some even said I was mad. Now, I can tell you that you were all wrong! Ha-ha!"

A murmur of excitement swept through the crowd. The photographers readied their cameras. "For I, Jeremy Olivier Bernardo Barracus Ignatius Englebert Snotgrass, have tracked down the legendary Yeti, captured it and smuggled it back into this country. I've

brought it here to show to the whole world. So that I could prove to you that the legend is in fact real."

The crowd gasped. Everyone had forgotten about the wedding now. "Ladies and gentlemen, members of the press, people of the world, I give you the famous Yeti....."

With a dramatic movement Great Uncle Jeremy pulled the cord and the curtains drew back.

Chapter Eleven

And Yeti again....

The crowd stopped in mid gasp. Behind the curtain stood what looked like a very big man wearing a brown suit and a kipper tie and holding a bunch of flowers.

"Eh?" said everyone, puzzled. A worried look came across Great Uncle Jeremy's face, and he turned and saw for himself what everyone else could see.

"What?" he cried. "You again!" He shot a fierce look at Brian and Pippa.

"That's him, I promise," said Brian. "Look closer." Great Uncle Jeremy adjusted his cracked monocle and looked at the man in the suit more closely. Only now did he see though the disguise. Only now did he realise that the Yeti had been there all along.

"But, of course!" he said. He turned to the crowd. "This *is* the Yeti. It is, really."

"We don't believe you," said one of the press photographers. "He looks like a man in a suit. He looks more human than you, in fact." There was a chorus of agreement from the others.

"This is a hoax, isn't it?" said a reporter.

"This is a hoot!" laughed Uncle George.

"Hey you," shouted another of the reporters to the Yeti. "You're not a Yeti, are you?"

"NUTS!" cried the Yeti.

"But, he IS a Yeti," cried Great Uncle Jeremy.

"Let me get this straight," said the same reporter. "You're standing there in a dressing gown and a pair of pink flip-flops, and you expect us to believe that the man over there is a Yeti?"

Great Uncle Jeremy turned to the Yeti and pleaded with him.

"Do something. Prove to them that you're a Yeti. Eat the flowers, jump up and swing from the roof, anything! Please!"

"MONKEYS!" cried the Yeti with a broad smile.

"Is this part of the entertainment?" said one wedding guest.

"The guy in the suit is quite good. Is he a comedian?" said someone else.

"He's hilarious!" cried Uncle George, tears of laughter streaming down his face.

"What's this fellow's name?" said another man. "I want to book him for my wedding too."

"DAVID ATTENBOROUGH!" slobbered the Yeti.

For the reporters and photographers from the press enough was enough. They all grabbed their equipment and started to leave.

Tonga's new husband, his face white with panic, rushed for the door along with them. "I'm off. Maybe I can still get this wedding annulled!" he cried.

"My perfect day is ruined! Ruined!" screeched Tonga as she stormed out of the marquee after him, with her sisters chasing behind.

"Please come back everyone! He IS a Yeti! Please believe me!" cried Great Uncle Jeremy, as the reporters and the wedding guests drifted away. But, nobody was listening to him any more. The only people left were Pippa and Brian, who beamed with triumph.

"It looks like you've lost," said Brian.

"That's what you get for being a big bully," said Pippa.

Great Uncle Jeremy's moustache trembled with rage and his face was bright purple.

"You've spoiled everything for me you pair of anacondas!"

"You can't blame us!" said Brian. "We did our bit. We got him behind the curtain like you asked." "Yes, so you can't evict us," said Pippa.

"Oh, can't I?"

Mum appeared at Brian and Pippa's side, rolling up her sleeves and eyeing him like a hawk eyes up its lunch. "Evict who, sorry?"

The two adults stood eye to eye for a moment, but it was Great Uncle Jeremy who blinked first. In fact, he positively shrank. Mum could outstare anyone.

"Very well. But I'll get even with you two, just wait."

He wheeled round in his flip-flops and stormed out of the tent. Brian and Pippa cheered.

"Well, we saved our Yeti," said Brian. "But now what are we going to do with him?"

"Come on, let's take him home," said Pippa.

They each took one of the Yeti's hands and led him out of the tent. Unfortunately they forgot to make sure he ducked this time. They were half way down the street before they realised that Yeti was wearing the marquee, bandana style, and the whole thing, including the tables and chairs, the vol-au-vents, the punchbowl, the vicar and the band, was dragging behind them.

The end

Granny Nothing
Catherine MacPhail

A warm-hearted, laugh-out-loud read from multi award-winning author Catherine MacPhail.

It is a dark and stormy night...

Nanny Sue is trying to get rid of Stephanie, Ewen and Baby Thomas so she can settle down to watch Star-Maker, her favourite TV programme. Nanny Sue's got ambitions to be a pop star, more fool her.

Then comes a banging on the door. It's loud enough to wake the dead. "It's the Bogeyman, come to get you!" shrieks Nanny Sue. (She's good with kids.)

But it is far worse than that. It is Granny Nothing, looking like a rhinoceros in a frock, dripping wet and complaining about her feet. And from this point on, things in the McAllister household will never be the same again...

Anyone for a worm sandwich?

ISBN 978-1-905537-31-0
Paperback, RRP £6.99
ISBN 978-1-905537-50-1
Ebook

The King of the Copper Mountains
Paul Biegel

Featured in *1001 Children's Books You Must Read Before You Grow Up*

The award-winning, timeless children's classic

At the end of his thousand-year reign of the Copper Mountains, old King Mansolain is tired and his heart is slowing down. When his attendant, the Hare, consults The Wonder Doctor, he is told he must keep the King engaged in life by telling him a story every night until the Doctor can find a cure.

The search is on for a nightly story more wonderful than the last, and one by one the kingdom's inhabitants arrive with theirs; the ferocious Wolf, the lovesick Donkey, the fire-breathing, three-headed Dragon. Last to arrive is the Dwarf with four ancient books and a prophecy that the King will live for another thousand years – but only if the Wonder Doctor returns in time.

'One of the blazing jewels of children's literature.'
The Sunday Times

ISBN 978-1-905537-14-3
Paperback, RRP £6.99

Wolfie
Emma Barnes

Lucie has always longed
for a dog.

But not one *this* big.

Or with such sharp teeth.

Or with such a hungry look
in its eyes.

Lucie realises her new pet is not a
dog...but *a wolf*. Not only that, but
a wolf with magical powers.

A talking wolf is not an easy
thing to hide from your family
and friends. Or from the bully
next door. And as Lucie grows to
love Wolfie, she also realises that
her new companion is in terrible
danger...

ISBN 978-1-905537-27-3
Paperback, RRP £6.99
ISBN 978-1-905537-67-9
Ebook

Jessica Haggerthwaite: Witch Dispatcher

Emma Barnes

Jessica has always planned to be a world-famous scientist one day. But her mother has decided to become a professional witch!

Who will take Jessica seriously now?

To stop her mother wrecking her plans (and breaking up the family), Jessica resolves to show her that no one needs to believe in magic these days. But her plans – like her mother's spells – don't always have the desired effect...

ISBN 978-1-905537-30-3
Paperback, RRP £6.99
ISBN 978-1-905537-54-9
Ebook

ILLUSTRATED BY
Emma Chichester Clark

How (Not) To Make Bad Children Good
Emma Barnes

Ever since she bit Father
Christmas when she was six
months old, it's been downhill all
the way for Martha Bones. She is
horrible to her baby brother Boris
and elder sister Sally, and her
parents are in despair.

Far away from Earth, Martha's
behaviour comes to the attention
of the Interstellar Agency whose
aim is to make bad children good.
Fred, an Interstellar agent with a
poor track record, is sent to Earth
as Martha's guardian agent. His
mission – to make Martha good.
But Martha has other ideas!

ISBN 978-1-905337-28-0
Paperback, RRP £6.99
ISBN 978-1-905537-65-5
Ebook

DarkIsle
D A Nelson

Ten-year-old Morag is being
held prisoner until a resourceful
dodo and a talking rat accidentally
rescue her. She jumps at
the chance to join them on
a dangerous mission to retrieve
an ancient stone that protects
their northern homeland.

The stone's thief is hiding off
the west coast of Scotland. And
only a stone dragon knows how
to find him.

Together, these four friends
journey to a mysterious island
beyond the horizon, where
danger and glory await. Along
the way she finds clues to the
disappearance of her parents
ten years before.

ISBN 978-1-905537-05-1
hardback, RRP £12.99
ISBN 978-1-905537-04-4
paperback, RRP £6.99
ISBN 978-1-905537-47-1
ebook

The exciting sequel to the bestselling *DarkIsle*

DarkIsle: Resurrection
D A Nelson

Two months after saving The Eye of Lornish, Morag is adjusting to life in the secret northern kingdom of Marnoch Mor.

But dark dreams are troubling her and a spate of unexplained events prove that even with the protection of her friends – Shona the dragon, Bertie the dodo and Aldiss the rat – Morag is still not safe from harm...

ISBN 978-1-905537-18-1
paperback, RRP £6.99
ISBN 978-1-905537-49-5
ebook

DarkIsle: The Final Battle
D A Nelson

All seems well in Marnoch Mor.
Bertie the dodo, Aldis the rat and
Shona the dragon are looking
forward to a relaxing Christmas.

However, Morag is having bad
dreams – an old enemy is trying
to reach her.

And when another former foe
turns up on her doorstep it is clear
something is badly wrong.

Morag and her friends are soon
forced to try and stand up to a
powerful new threat, one more
terrifying than they have ever
encountered before.

The battle for the DarkIsle of
Murst must be won...or Marnoch
Mor itself will be lost.

ISBN 978-1-905537-95-2
Paperback, RRP £6.99
ISBN 978-1-905537-68-6
Ebook

Lee and the Consul Mutants
Keith Charters

Former no.1 in The Herald's Children's Bestseller chart

It's not every day that a part of your body explodes. But Lee's appendix does just that, landing him in hospital.

After his operation, Lee discovers that being in hospital has its bright side. But his world turns dark again when he uncovers a fiendish plot by the white-coated Consul Mutants to *take over the world.*

Other kids might quake in their boots at this news, but not Lee. He's determined to save the planet and formulates a cunning plan to stop the alien invasion.

Lee & the Consul Mutants is the story of a fearless boy battling against intergalactic odds for the sake of mankind. Lee's only weapon is his intelligence…which is a pity.

ISBN 978-1-905537-24-2
Paperback, RRP £6.99
ISBN 978-1-905537-42-6
Ebook

Lee Goes For Gold
Keith Charters

Meeting his dad's multizillionaire
employer inspires Lee to come
up with a brilliant get-rich-quick
scheme of his own.

But not everyone is keen for Lee to
succeed. Local shopkeeper Panface
certainly isn't, and it seems that
he has sneaky spies out there,
trying to ruin Lee's plans.

Will Lee overcome those out to
stop him making his fortune?
Or will he spend the whole time
daydreaming about how many
houses he'll be able to own and
how many of them will have
swimming pools and butlers?

Lee will need to rely on his
common sense and financial
genius if he's to succeed…so it
could be an uphill struggle.

ISBN 978-1-905537-25-9
Paperback, RRP £6.99
ISBN 978-1-905537-43-3
Ebook

Lee Goes For Gold

Keith Chambers